NEARLY FEARLESS

MONKEY PIRATES

BATTLE OF THE
PIRATE
BANDS

A 4D BOOK

BY MICHAEL ANTHONY STEELE
ILLUSTRATED BY PAULINE REEVES

PICTURE WINDOW BOOKS
a capstone imprint

Nearly Fearless Monkey Pirates is published by Stone Arch Books,
A Capstone Imprint
1710 Roe Crest Drive
North Mankato, Minnesota 56003
www.capstonepub.com

Cataloging-in-Publication Data is available on the Library of Congress website.
ISBN: 978-1-5158-2679-8 (library binding)
ISBN: 978-1-5158-2687-3 (paperback)
ISBN: 978-1-5158-2691-0 (eBook PDF)

Summary: Pirates from across the seven seas are gathering for a great pirate
contest. But when the prize trophy is stolen, the Nearly Fearless Monkey
Pirates get wrongly blamed. The crew must find the missing prize, or they'll
meet a watery grave!

Designer: Ted Williams

Design elements
Shutterstock: Angeliki Vel, MAD SNAIL, nazlisart

Printed and bound in the USA
PA021

Download the Capstone 4D™ app!

- Ask an adult to download the Capstone 4D app.

- Scan the cover and stars inside the book for additional content.

When you scan a spread, you'll find
fun extra stuff to go with this book!
You can also find these things
on the web at www.capstone4D.com
using the password: pirate.26798

TABLE OF CONTENTS

CHAPTER 1
TARGET PRACTICE
PAGE 7

CHAPTER 2
VANISHING ACT
PAGE 14

CHAPTER 3
MONKEYS ON THE RUN
PAGE 19

CHAPTER 4
MONKEY MISSION
PAGE 27

CHAPTER 5
PIRATE PUNISHMENT
PAGE 35

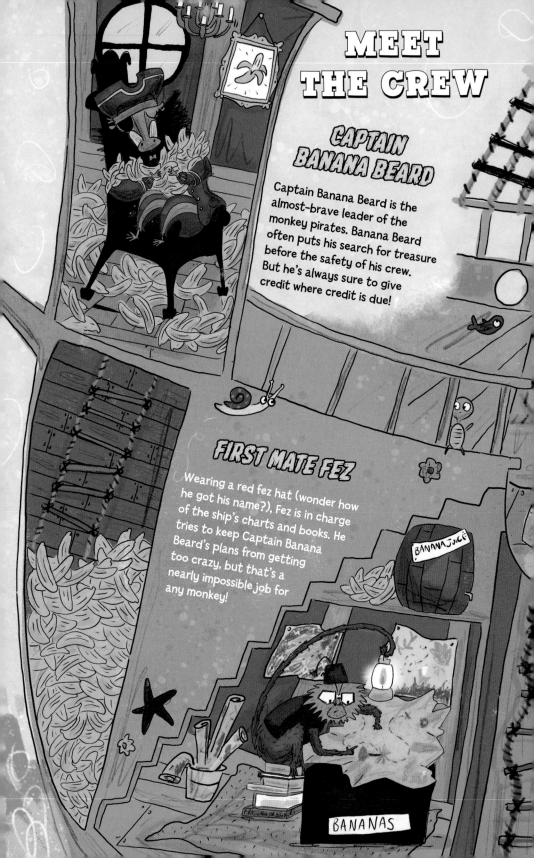

MEET THE CREW

CAPTAIN BANANA BEARD

Captain Banana Beard is the almost-brave leader of the monkey pirates. Banana Beard often puts his search for treasure before the safety of his crew. But he's always sure to give credit where credit is due!

FIRST MATE FEZ

Wearing a red fez hat (wonder how he got his name?), Fez is in charge of the ship's charts and books. He tries to keep Captain Banana Beard's plans from getting too crazy, but that's a nearly impossible job for any monkey!

BANANA JUICE

BANANAS

CREWMAN MR. PICKLES

Mr. Pickles is the lowest on the chain of command, but he's still excited to be the best pirate he can be. With every job he does, Mr. Pickles is one step closer to being a great pirate captain, just like his hero, Captain Banana Beard.

QUARTERMASTER FOSSEY

Fossey keeps track of the ship's goods and treasure. She's in charge of all the gear and knows the supplies down to the last banana. And if the adventure calls for a certain tool that the ship doesn't have, Fossey can build it in record time.

CHAPTER 1
TARGET PRACTICE

Mr. Pickles ran onto the deck of the monkey pirates' ship, the *Merry Monkey*. He held a set of bongos. "I'm all set," he said.

Fossey shook her head. "I'll explain this one more time," she said. "It's not that kind of battle of the bands."

"It's not bands that play music, but bands of pirates," Fez added. "You know? Different groups of pirates."

"Crews from all around compete in different challenges," Fossey explained. "The winners are the best pirates in the world."

Mr. Pickles sighed. "So . . . not even a karaoke night?"

"No!" shouted Fez and Fossey.

Just then, Captain Banana Beard yelled from the other side of the deck. "Ready the cannon," he ordered.

Fez, Fossey, and Mr. Pickles ran to their captain. They swiftly loaded one of the ship's cannons.

"Fire!" shouted the captain.

Fossey fired the cannon. **BOOM!**

A coconut sailed over the water. It zoomed toward a ring floating on a barrel. The coconut zipped through the ring and splashed into the water. **SWISH-SPLASH!**

"Ahoy!" shouted the captain.
"A yo-ho-hole in one!"

"Yay!" cheered his crew.

Next it was the other pirates'
turns. The elephant pirates stood
in their ship nearby. Their ship
barely floated because of its four
heavy crew members.

They fired a giant peanut-
brittle ball. **SPLOOSH!** It missed
the target.

The giraffe pirates fired a head of cabbage. **SPLASH!** They missed too.

"Fire!" shouted Captain Feather Beak—the captain of the chicken pirates. They shot an egg out over the water. **SPLAT!** It smashed against the side of the target.

Captain Squeaks McGee raised his sword. "Fire!" he squeaked.

The tiny mouse pirate ship fired a cheese ball. **Ploop!** It plopped into the water only a foot away. It was so quiet that no one noticed.

Just then, a large ship sailed up to the *Merry Monkey*. The *Salty Dog* was home to the dog pirates.

Their captain was a big bulldog. She was also Captain Banana Beard's personal bully— Captain Viola Belle.

"Well, if it isn't my good old friend," said Viola. "Captain Banana Bread."

Banana Beard shook with anger and said, "It's Banana Beard! Banana Beard!" Several bananas fell from his beard.

Viola rolled her eyes.

"Whatevs," she said. "Let me show you how it's done." She turned to her crew. "Fire!"

The *Salty Dog's* cannon roared. **BOOM!** A large tennis ball shot out across the water. It swished through the hole in the target. **SWISH-SPLASH!**

Viola grinned at Banana Beard and said, "And *that's* how we win the battle . . . every year!"

CHAPTER 2
VANISHING ACT

All the pirate ships floated next to Admiral Tusk's ship. The Admiral flopped onto the deck to greet them.

"Well done, everyone!" the walrus said. "But there are two clear leaders. The *Merry Monkey* and the *Salty Dog*."

The Admiral's crew, the navy seals, clapped their flippers together.

The walrus raised a flipper and they stopped. "Now it's time for the next challenge!" he said.

"Begging the admiral's pardon," Captain Viola called. "But could we get another look at the trophy?" She grinned at her crew. "I'm building a new trophy case. I want to make sure it's big enough."

The dog pirates laughed.

"I don't see why not," replied the admiral. He nodded at the navy seals. They shuffled to the center of the ship.

"Don't listen to her, mateys," Banana Beard told his crew. "She be trying to upset us."

The seals neared a tall object covered with a sheet. They pulled away the cloth. There was no trophy—only a wooden barrel.

All of the pirates gasped.

"The trophy's been stolen!" Viola shouted. "Who could've done such a thing?"

One of the seals reached in the barrel and pulled out a banana. "It's full of bananas, Admiral," she cried.

Everyone looked at the Nearly Fearless Monkey Pirates.

"I can't believe you would stoop so low, Banana Brat," said Viola.

Captain Banana Beard shook with anger. "I would never steal the trophy," he said. "And it's Banana Beard! Banana Beard!"

Two bananas fell from his
bushy beard.

Admiral Tusk glared at
Banana Beard. "It's time for the
next pirate challenge." He pointed
a flipper at the *Merry Monkey*. "Get
those monkey pirates!"

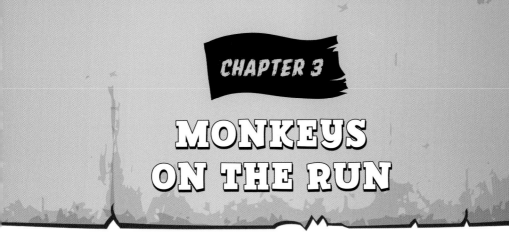

CHAPTER 3

MONKEYS ON THE RUN

BOOM! BOOM-BOOM!

Cannons roared all around the monkey pirates. They ducked as cabbages, tennis balls, and eggs flew in from all sides.

POP. POP-POP. POP.

Several cheese balls bounced off the side of the monkeys' ship. No one seemed to notice.

"Set sail, mateys!" Captain
Banana Beard ordered.

The monkey pirates sprang into
action. They started raising sails
and pulled up the anchor. Soon the
Merry Monkey sped away from the
other pirates.

"Why are we running,
Captain?" asked Fossey. "We
didn't steal anything."

"I need time to think," replied the captain. "And I need us to sail faster!" He held tight to the ship's wheel. "Faster!"

Fez, Fossey, and Mr. Pickles raised another sail. The ship picked up speed.

The *Merry Monkey* sped across the sea. The *Salty Dog* sailed close behind.

Not all of the ships were fast. The elephant pirates were too heavy. Their ship barely moved at all.

The mouse pirate ship was too tiny. It took a long time to sail over each little wave. The chicken pirate ship was a little bigger. But it didn't stand a chance against the others.

The giraffe pirate ship, the *Sore Throat*, was a different story.

It followed close behind the *Merry Monkey* and the *Salty Dog.*

"Heads up, mateys," said Captain Stiffneck, the giraffe pirate captain. "Secret weapon time!"

The giraffes hung sails from their long necks. Four more sails meant they could catch more wind. More wind meant more speed. The *Sore Throat* sped past the *Salty Dog.* It closed in on the *Merry Monkey.*

Suddenly the wind shifted. The sails wrapped around the giraffes' heads so they couldn't see. The *Sore Throat* turned out to open sea.

"Just you and me, Banana Brains!" shouted Captain Viola. The *Salty Dog* closed in.

"Yo-ho-hold onto your hat, Viola," said Captain Banana Beard. "We have a secret weapon of our own!" He turned to his crew. "Time for a tailwind, mateys!"

Fez, Fossey, and Mr. Pickles ran to the back of the ship. They hung over the side and sat in the water.

Then they spun their tails
around and around. They spun
them so fast that they made three
monkey-tail propellers!

The *Merry Monkey* picked up speed. It raced away from the *Salty Dog*.

BOOM! A canon roared from the *Salty Dog*. A large tennis ball slammed into the back of the *Merry Monkey*. Fez, Fossey, and Mr. Pickles ran for cover.

The dog pirates closed in.

Captain Viola grinned. "No more monkey business."

CHAPTER 4

MONKEY MISSION

BOOM!

Another giant tennis ball hit
the monkeys' main sail. It became
tangled in the large cloth. The
Merry Monkey slowed. The *Salty
Dog* closed in.

"We don't have much time,"
said Captain Banana Beard. He
turned to his crew. "First Mate Fez,
I need a volunteer from the crew."

Fez turned to Fossey. "Captain needs a volunteer from the crew."

Fossey turned to the only one left—Mr. Pickles. "Any volunteers?"

Mr. Pickles shrugged and said, "I volunteer, Captain."

"That's a good lad," said the captain. "I have an important mission for you. Find out who stole that trophy."

Mr. Pickles saluted. "Aye-aye, Captain!"

BAM! The ship shook beneath their feet. The *Salty Dog* scraped up against the *Merry Monkey*.

"You can run but you can't hide, Banana Boy!" shouted Captain Viola.

Viola and the dog pirates jumped onto the *Merry Monkey*. They drew their long swords.

"We're under attack!" shouted Banana Beard. He drew his own sword.

Fez drew his sword. Fossey drew her sword. Mr. Pickles ran to the side of the ship. He jumped overboard.

SPLOOSH!

Viola gave a deep belly laugh. "Such a brave crew," she said. "You should be captain of the *chicken* pirates!"

Captain Viola crossed swords with Captain Banana Beard. Fez fought with one of the dog pirates. Fossey battled the other two, holding one sword with her tail.

KLINK! KLANK! KLINK!

Suddenly the other pirate ships arrived. Everyone was there except the mouse pirates. Their ship hadn't made it over the first wave. No one seemed to notice.

The ships surrounded the *Merry Monkey*. The monkey pirates were trapped. Admiral Tusk and his navy seals shuffled aboard. They drew their own swords.

"Stand down, Banana Beard!" shouted the admiral.

Captain Banana Beard sighed. There was no escape. He threw his sword to the deck. Fez and Fossey did the same.

CHAPTER 5

PIRATE PUNISHMENT

"Walk the plank! Walk the plank!" chanted all of the pirates.

A long plank of wood was nailed to the *Salty Dog*. It jutted out over the water.

Captain Banana Beard walked out to the end. Captain Viola pointed her sword at him. Fez and Fossey watched with the rest of the pirates.

"In you go, Captain Banana Breath," said Viola.

Banana Beard trembled with anger. "It's Beard! Banana Beard!" Two bananas fell from his beard.

Admiral Tusk held up a flipper for silence. "Do you have any last words, Captain?"

"Aye," replied Banana Beard. He gazed out at all the pirates. "'Twas not me who stole the trophy," he said. "But think on this. We all be fierce pirates. Should we really punish a pirate who did such a fearless thing?

Should that pirate have to walk the plank?"

The surrounding pirates glanced at each other. Some scratched their heads in thought. Then they all glared at Captain Banana Beard and shouted, "Yes!"

Banana Beard shrugged and said, "'Twas worth a try."

Viola inched forward. "Time for a swim," she said. She jabbed at him with her sword.

"Wait a minute!" a distant
voice called.

Everyone turned to the *Salty
Dog's* main hatch. The doors
swung open.

"Look what I found below
deck," said Mr. Pickles. He shuffled
out carrying a huge trophy.

Everyone gasped.

"Captain Viola!" shouted the admiral. "You stole the trophy!"

"Forget what I said before," said Captain Banana Beard. "She should definitely walk the plank for that."

Captain Viola Belle growled. "You first, Banana . . . Banana . . ."

She charged at him. Then she stepped on one of the fallen bananas. Her feet slipped out from under her.

"WHOA!" Viola fell off the plank into the water. **SPLOOSH!**

Captain Banana Beard strolled
back to the ship. He picked up the
other banana and tucked it into
his beard. "It's Banana Beard,"
he said.

Admiral took the trophy from Mr. Pickles. He handed it to Banana Beard. "Congratulations," he said. "The monkey pirates win the Battle of the Pirate Bands!"

"Yay!" the pirates cheered.

Fez, Fossey, and Mr. Pickles stood proudly by their captain. Banana Beard raised his hands, and called out, "I say we have a yo-ho-hoedown!"

The pirates cheered again.

And the mouse pirates arrived just in time for the party, but no one seemed to notice.

ABOUT THE AUTHOR

Michael Anthony Steele has been in the entertainment industry for more than twenty years. He has worked in several capacities of film and television production from props and special effects all the way up to writing and directing. For many years, Mr. Steele has written exclusively for family entertainment. For television and video, he wrote for shows including *WISHBONE*, *Barney & Friends*, and *Boz, The Green Bear Next Door*. He has authored more than one hundred books for various characters and brands including *Batman*, *Green Lantern*, *LEGO City*, *Spider-Man*, *The Hardy Boys*, *Garfield*, and *Night at the Museum*.

ABOUT THE ILLUSTRATOR

Pauline Reeves lives by the sea in southwest England, with her husband, two children, and dog Jenson. She has loved drawing and creating since she was a child. Following her passion, Ms. Reeves graduated from Plymouth College of Art with a degree in illustration, and she specializes in children's literature. She takes inspiration from the funny and endearing things animals and people do every day. Ms. Reeves works both digitally and with traditional materials to create quirky illustrations with humor and charm.

GLOSSARY

admiral (AD-muh-ruhl)—an officer of high ranking in the navy or coast guard

bongos (BONG-gohs)—a pair of small drums that are joined together and played with the hands

fierce (FEERSS)—daring and dangerous

karaoke (kah-ree-OH-kee)—an activity where people sing the words of popular songs while a machine plays the background music

mission (MISH-uhn)—a planned job

overboard (OH-vur-BORD)—over the side of a ship into the water

propeller (pro-PEL-ur)—a rotating blade that moves a vehicle

saluted (suh-LOO-ted)—raised the right hand to the forehead as a sign of respect

1. You read that Captain Viola is Captain Banana Beard's "personal bully." What makes her a bully?

2. Captain Viola said Banana Beard stole the trophy. Do you think she really believed that, or was she telling a lie? How can you tell?

FOR YOUR PIRATE LOG

1. Create your own animal-pirate crew. Draw a picture of the captain, crew, and ship, and label them all with their names.

2. At the pirate contest, we only hear about the cannon event. What are some other events or challenges that could happen at a pirate contest? Make a list.

3. What do you think would have happened if the trophy hadn't been found? Write a different ending for the book.

THE SHIP DOESN'T STOP HERE!

Discover more at
www.capstonekids.com

- VIDEOS & CONTESTS
- GAMES & PUZZLES
- FRIENDS & FAVORITES
- AUTHORS & ILLUSTRATORS

Find cool websites and more books like this one at **www.facthound.com**.
Just type in the Book ID: 9781515826798 and you're ready to go!